POKÉMON
ALOLA REGION
ACTIVITY BOOK

PIKACHU PRESS ™

TABLE OF CONTENTS

POKéMON™
ALOLA REGION
ACTIVITY BOOK

PIKACHU PRESS™

$12.99 USA
$15.50 CAN

The Pokémon Company
INTERNATIONAL

Publisher: Heather Dalgleish
Art Director: Chris Franc
Design Manager: Kevin Lalli
Designer: Justin Gonyea
Writer: Lawrence Neves
Editor: Wolfgang Baur
Merchandise Development Manager: Eoin Sanders
Merchandise Development: Hank Woon
Project Manager: Emily Luty

The Pokémon Company International
10400 NE 4th Street, Suite 2800
Bellevue, WA 98004 USA
Printed in Shenzhen, China

First printing June 2017.

This book was produced by Quarto Publishing Group USA Inc.
ISBN: 978-1-60438-195-5

FSC
www.fsc.org

MIX
Paper from
responsible sources
FSC® C017606

MELEMELE
ISLAND

Welcome to Melemele Island, one of the four islands of the Alola region! It is located in the northwest of the Alola island chain, and houses some fascinating Pokémon. The guardian tapu for Melemele is Tapu Koko—will you meet Tapu Koko in your journey through Melemele? We think you might!

CROSSWORD CHALLENGE

Can you help this first partner Pokémon find out all about its friends in Melemele? See if you have the knowledge to help Rowlet find its way around by learning about which Pokémon you befriend—and which to avoid!

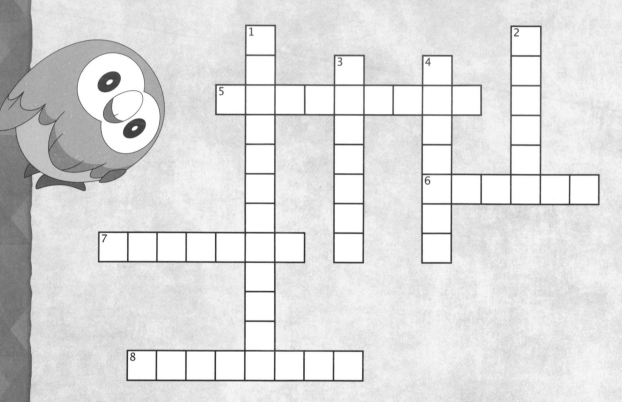

ACROSS

5. This Pokémon's beak can achieve temperatures of over 200 degrees Fahrenheit.

6. Trainers often have a hard time getting this solitary Pokémon to trust them.

7. They can drill into the side of a tree at the rate of 16 pecks per second.

8. It's a natural enemy of Rattata, though the two rarely interact because they're awake at different times.

DOWN

1. This Pokémon is very vain about the golden Charm on its forehead, and becomes enraged if any dirt dulls its bright surface.

2. During the day, this Pokémon rests and generates energy via photosynthesis.

3. It can throw sharp-edge feathers, known as blade quills, with great accuracy.

4. This Pokémon uses the water balloons it blows from its nose as a weapon in battle.

ANSWERS ON PAGE 90

POKÉMON CHECKLIST

Hey Pokémon fans! Test your skills at identifying Pokémon when hidden among their friends! Take a good look at this Pokémon collage and see if you can find the Pokémon listed below! An extra ten points if you can find this scrambled Pokémon!

XDRTAIR

1. When night comes, this Pokémon immediately falls asleep no matter where it may be.

2. It shows off its dancing ability when trying to cheer up its Trainer.

3. It stores berry seeds in its beak to use as ammunition.

4. When it spits flames, the fiery bell at this Pokémon's throat begins to ring.

5. It can surf on its own tail, standing on the flat surface and using psychic power to raise itself off the ground.

ANSWERS ON PAGE 90

WEIGHT FOR IT

Decidueye is a winged menace when angered, but it can't achieve liftoff unless it makes accommodations for weight and mass and velocity… and well, everything really! Check page 89 for a list of Pokémon weights and heights.

Let's start by calculating the difference between Decidueye and Rowlet's weight:

Rowlet's weight is:
A) 2.3 lbs.
B) 3.2 lbs.
C) 3.3 lbs.

Decideueye's weight is:
A) 80.7 lbs.
B) 78.0 lbs.
C) 87.7 lbs.

The weight difference is_____.

Now, which of these Pokémon comes closest to this weight?

ANSWERS ON PAGE 90

IT TAKES ALL TYPES

Litten needs help to identify certain friends and foes—and it is going to start by correctly classifying these dual-type Pokémon by their types. See if you can help Litten by drawing a line between the Pokémon and its type. Good luck!

NORMAL
FLYING

WATER

WATER
FAIRY

DARK
NORMAL

GRASS
GHOST

FIRE
DARK

ANSWERS ON PAGE 90

WHO'S THAT POKÉMON?

Torracat attacks with its front legs—but it doesn't just go after any Pokémon. Help Torracat identify rookie from rival by identifying these Pokémon from their silhouettes. Try to do so in 90 seconds or less, or Torracat may end up tangling with the wrong Pokémon!

1

2

3

4

5

6

ANSWERS ON PAGE 90

POKÉMON NAME GAME

Everyone knows that Incineroar is touchy—if not in the right mood, it will ignore you. Keep Incineroar engaged by playing this name game with it. The rules for this one-player, two-player or multiplayer game are simple.

RULES

You and a friend pick out a final Evolution Pokémon like Incineroar. Each of you then writes that Pokémon's name down on a piece of paper. Now come up with as many words as you can using that Pokémon's letters within a two minute limit. The player with the most words after two minutes wins.

Example:

INCINEROAR

Roar

Crone

Ice

One

ODD POKÉMON OUT

Popplio feels lonely—it knows its own type, but you have to help it find other similar Pokémon. Match Popplio with the Pokémon of the same type on the right, and let's make sure Popplio feels comfortable with these Pokémon.

ANSWERS ON PAGE 90

CRYPTOGLYPHICS

Can you help us find out who this mysterious Melemele Pokémon is? Decipher the clues below and use the cryptographic to solve this puzzle.

[I]T P[E]LTS [I]TS [O]PP[O]N[E]NTS W[I]TH

WAT[E][R] [B]ALL[O][O]NS [I]N A SW[I]FT

AND SK[I]LLFUL [B]ATTLE DANC[E].

ITS NAME IS [B][R][I][O]NN[E].

LEGEND

= B

= I

= O

= R

= E

 is not repeated.

ANSWERS ON PAGE 90

MELEMELE ISLAND

WORD SEARCH

We have a special request–a Trainer has asked that we help identify a Pokémon she's lost. They became good friends, but with all the excitement surrounding Pokémon training on Melemele, she turned her back for a minute and it was gone! You can help by finding the following Pokémon in the word search below. Then take all the letters highlighted in red and help spell out the missing Pokémon. She will be eternally grateful for your help!

```
U V P T X C U G B N U O U J Z M O W I G
E K F L D R N N O H H K H A L H R G C J
T M O K N O H V A B H O L B D C O P J Y
Y R S T G W F G P R I M A R I N A L C R
T C M T G L O X G T D E C I D U E Y E V
R R T P L E R S E S Z V C E T V U T D
D X P R I T M V D O G K I N W O R N I Z
N R V O C K S O O I T M N T X R K G M H
M F D I P G I H Q S P O C C W R A O U K
J G W N N P S P D K I B I D M A B O C T
G B T P N M L K E R F E N L H C F S D J
R C F L U Y D I B K Q E E Z I A K Z X J
N A N G F C L L O K D C R D G T U N G E
J D A R T R I X M A Z O O L X W T R H G
O J H M U E J H U K R P A R J F J E M O
W X T T V B N Q N N E J R K Z R Z K N V
```

ROWLET
DARTRIX
DECIDUEYE

LITTEN
TORRACAT
INCINEROAR

POPPLIO
BRIONNE
PIKIPEK

YUNGOOS
GUMSHOOS

Missing Pokémon: _____

ANSWERS ON PAGE 90

WHO'S THAT POKÉMON?

Another Trainer, another lost Pokémon! Help this Trainer find his Pokémon by identifying these Pokémon by their Evolutions. The last missing Pokémon on this list is the one we're looking for. Fill in its name and give yourself an extra pat on the back for being such a great help on Melemele.

_____ Datrix Deuicdeye

Litten Torroacht Incineroar

Poppolio Brionne Primarina

Pipikek Trumbeak Toucannon

ANSWER: Pipikek

ANSWERS ON PAGE 90

WEIGHT FOR IT

A sailboat from Melemele may sink into the sea! They say that the weight of the Pokémon on board cannot exceed 1,000 pounds in any one area at a time. Let's see if we can prove them wrong. If you had the following groups of Pokémon, which ones' weight would add up closest to 1,000 pounds? Check out page 89 for a list of Pokémon heights and weights.

10 Decidueye — *90*

10 Primarina — *97*

10 Incineroar — *183*

100 Litten — *9.5*

50 Popplio — *16.5*

MELEMELE ISLAND

ANSWER ON PAGE 91

RING AROUND THE COLORS

Training on Melemele can be distracting, what with all the tropical colors and beautiful Pokémon. How good are you at seeing past the camouflage and identifying Pokémon–simply by remembering their colors? Let's try with Toucannon. Using the illustration below, see if you can guess the missing color on Toucannon by picking from the choices on the left. You can do this!

OPTIONS:

Green

Red

Blue

Yellow

ANSWER ON PAGE 91

MELEMELE ISLAND

SPOT THE DIFFERENCE

Yungoos is constantly on the move during the day, so it's hard to get a read on this elusive Pokémon. At night, different story—but you may not get a chance at finding one! See if you can tell the difference, and find which of these Yungoos is the real deal.

ANSWER ON PAGE 91

TIME TRAVELER

Gumshoos displays amazing patience when it's on a stakeout. It's a natural enemy of Rattata, but the two rarely interact because they're awake at different times. Find out if you'll spot one awake before 6 P.M. by playing the simple game below.

You spot a Gumshoos at 3:00 P.M.

Twenty minutes later, you lose the Gumshoos and spot a Dartrix.

You follow the Dartrix for forty minutes, and then take a 15 minute break.

One hour later, you pick up the trail of the Gumshoos.

You follow the Gumshoos, but it hides in some tall grass, and you spend nearly 35 minutes looking for it.

When you see it again, it looks sleepy.

You break for dinner, because you're famished, and start out again 15 minutes later.

You spot the Gumshoos. Did you make it before your 6:00 P.M. deadline?

ANSWER ON PAGE 91

MELEMELE ISLAND

SURF TIME!

Alolan Raichu is ready to surf on its own tail! But how high can Alolan Raichu go before it wipes out? Here's a fun way to find out. Arrange the following Pokémon found on Melemele Island in order from tallest to shortest and bring Alolan Raichu back down to the ground! Check out page 89 for a list of Pokémon heights and weights.

ANSWERS ON PAGE 91

POKÉMON ACROSTICS

Let's see how creative you can be with Pokémon names.
Play this game with one, two or three players.

RULES

Pick a Pokémon name. Write the name in a column. If you
pick a Pokémon like Alolan Meowth, you should have a
column that looks like this. Now, spell the longest word
you can with the letters in each row. For example, starting
with the first letter, try to spell the longest word you can
with A like "arterial". You can only make one word per row,
but you get a point for each letter in the word.

A _____

L _____

O _____

L _____

A _____

N _____

M _____

E _____

O _____

W _____

T _____

H _____

BONUS: Time the game and see how many words you can make
in two minutes. Give yourself an extra five points per line for
spelling Pokémon names!

PARTS NOT INCLUDED

Finally, we've come to the guardian of Melemele Island. Tapu Koko has a short attention span, but don't ever underestimate it, as it is quick to anger. See if you can help it before it becomes angry, and before it forgets that it's angry. Help by identifying these Pokémon simply by their appendages, like claws, feathers, and skin. See if you can identify all six!

MELEMELE ISLAND

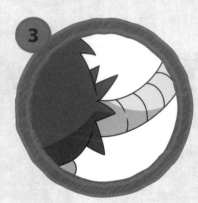

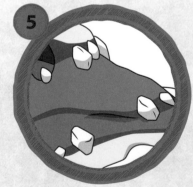

ANSWERS ON PAGE 91

AKALA
ISLAND

Beautiful and lush Akala Island is in the northeast of the Alola Island chain, and is home to more incredible Pokémon. See if you can spot some of the creepy crawlers, and the sage swingers of the jungle canopy. Enjoy your time here!

CODE POKÉMON

What better way to introduce you to Akala Island than by uncovering one of its mysterious Pokémon—a Pokémon that lives at the bottom of the sea and is attracted to the bright coral of Corsola. Who could this Pokémon be?
In each of the letters below is a Pokémon. Color in those Pokémon by using the key below, and it will spell out the Pokémon you seek!

____ ____ ____ ____ ____ ____ ____ ____

ANSWERS ON PAGE 91

POKÉMON CHECKLIST

Do you have everything you need for your journey into Akala? How about a rounded knowledge of all the Pokémon you'll find? Take a good look at this Pokémon collage and see if you can find the Pokémon listed below! An extra ten points if you can find this scrambled Pokémon!

EAXXPOT

1. This Pokémon sleeps the day away, basking in the sunlight.

2. It uses the water bubble that surrounds its head as a weapon.

3. All of these Pokémon are female, and tend to attract male Salandit and live in a group.

4. The flaming bone this Pokémon spiwns like a baton once belonged to its mother.

5. This Pokémon is both lively and cheerful, and often attracts a crowd of other Pokémon drawn to its energy and lovely scent.

ANSWERS ON PAGE 91

FINISH THIS POKÉMON

Dewpider spends a lot of time in the water—and all that water can really wash the color out of you. It's up to you to finish drawing this Dewpider—and then you can pick the correct color combination to complete it!

AKALA ISLAND

CHOOSE YOUR COLORS:

1) Green / Blue / Gray

2) Pink / Blue / Green

3) Blue / White / Red

ANSWER ON PAGE 91

WEIGHT FOR IT

Araquanid can use the bubble that surrounds its head as a shield to protect weaker opponents—but only so many Pokémon will be able to benefit from the protection at one time. Assuming that Araquanid can only protect up to 500 lbs. at a time, pick one of these groups of Pokémon that comes closest to 500 lbs.—without going over. Check out page 89 for a list of Pokémon heights and weights.

ANSWERS ON PAGE 91

POKÉMON CHECKLIST

Trainers should be aware at all times of the strengths and weaknesses of their Pokémon. They should also be able to identify Pokémon with minimal information—a quick mind in the field is a quick mind in battle. See if you can identify these Pokémon, and maybe the last one will come home with you if you give it a safe place to sleep.

1. This Pokémon gives off a strange flickering light.

2. This Pokémon gives off a toxic gas that causes dizziness and confusion when inhaled.

3. Its petals have evolved into a hard shell to protect its head and body from attackers.

4. Adding the flowers this Pokémon collects to bathwater makes for a relaxing soak.

5. It spends most of its time in the jungle canopy.

6. Sunbathers use the sticky slime on the outside of this Pokémon to soothe a sunburn. Gross.

7. During the night, this Pokémon seeks out a safe place to sleep for the next day.

ANSWERS ON PAGE 91

WALL SCRAWL

With all these new Pokémon in Alola, and especially on Akala, getting names right could mean the difference between befriending a Pokémon and offending a Pokémon. The trick is to say each name phonetically. Someone left behind the phonetic spelling of a couple of Pokémon—see if you can decipher them. Oh, and someone is looking for the last Pokémon on this list!

SHY KNOT ECK

DO PIE DER

PASS IM EYAN

PAHL O SAND

SAL AZ EL

LOOR RANT IZ

ANSWERS ON PAGE 91

POKÉMON SEEK AND FIND

Evolved Pokémon have their advantages. However, some Trainers don't like to evolve their Pokémon, while others prefer to catch the evolved form of Pokémon and train them from there. In the collage below, identify only those Pokémon that represent the last Evolution in their chain.

ANSWERS ON PAGE 91

IT TAKES ALL TYPES

Type match ups in Akala are tricky—lots of sea-worthy Pokémon that live in the water, and lots of plant-based Pokémon that live on land, many of which share similar types. But we're looking for something more specific from the Pokémon below—we want Pokémon that match at least one of Salazzle's types. Can you tell us which of the following make that match?

1

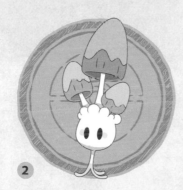

2

3

4

5

6

ANSWERS ON PAGE 92

AKALA ISLAND

WHO'S THAT POKÉMON?

Alolan Marowak feels deeply for fallen comrades—and it has seen a lot of Pokémon. Help Alolan Marowak identify these last few Pokémon that it recently said goodbye to on Akala Island so that it can move on and battle again.

1

2

3

4

5

6

7

8

9

ANSWERS ON PAGE 92

WORD SEARCH

Help us find the missing Pokémon by finding the Pokémon below, then taking the red letters and unscrambling them! Your help is greatly appreciated!

```
S S A N D Y G A S T N N N P J L W I Z T T V U E N
P A P K K T W R X F C I C O M F E Y H H O D H N V
F A L N B M U W I G G L Y T U F F O H D X P D F J
K R E A B A P P R K X D P U H F U Q C M F X E B F
T A U L Z C G Z S C Q X A S V V V J S F O W A E Z
T Q Q U O Z C N A X O I S F X W E O M L M M B R N
W U B R V K L N L Z D A S T H X V I V T A A R R A
O A N A K L R E A L Y Z I D T Y P Z K O N R K D Y
B N C N Z A O N N E W H M U S Q A F Y X T E F P C
M I E T X I V J D E F F I Q K V Q O Y A I A T A C
P D S I A D G J I F X O A V X T G O U P S N S L U
C X T S T N S X T L S P N P E B M R J E F I B O M
W E R O M Γ Z N S R T V G E Y A F A G X C E Q S J
N D N S T L W X J R I S W G G U S N R K P N H S B
I X X L T R Q X K P S A B Z R K G N T I X L A A
C I X X V E Y D L G N C L R S A C U Y Z Z H D N R
D L H U F O E O S U N T O Z E T T R M Z Q G L D B
Q L U C T T P N O E D J D Y E V U L U N S S J O
H A M U E G A B E S Q W H K A T N Z Z F K Z L C A
T U U M R A F H W E J E R S V Q O A W Z U U U M C
C P K Z N R E K Y N H Y P D E W P I D E R V I Z H
```

BARBOACH   **FOMANTIS**   **STEENEE**   **SANDYGAST**
MAREANIE   **LURANTIS**   **TSAREENA**   **PALOSSAND**
TOXAPEX   **SALANDIT**   **COMFEY**   **PYUKUMUKU**
DEWPIDER   **SALAZZLE**   **ORANGURU**
ARAQUANID   **WIGGLYTUFF**   **PASSIMIAN**

Missing Pokémon: ___ ___ ___ ___ ___ ___ ___ ___ ___ ___

ANIMATION PAGE 92

MAZE ME

Getting through a maze is definitely not easy, and no one is going to hand you a map. Let's try by following the natural Evolution of a Pokémon. Starting with Bounsweet, work through this maze to find Steenee, and soon you'll end up with Tsareena—and from there, there's more to explore on Akala Island!

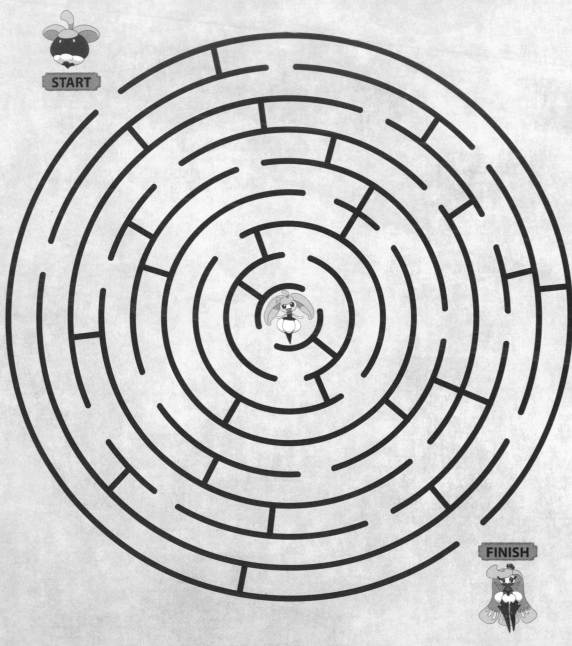

AKALA ISLAND

ANSWER ON PAGE 92

POKÉMON CHECKLIST

Once again, a Trainer needs help with his prized Pokémon. It's okay—you can show off a little and showcase your smarts while you help him look. Impress him with your knowledge of the following Pokémon, then let him know that you found his as well—it's the last Pokémon on this checklist!

1. The poisonous gas this Pokémon gives off contains powerful pheromones and is sometimes used as a perfume ingredient.

2. During the day, this Pokémon plants itself beside a tree to absorb nutrients from the roots while it naps.

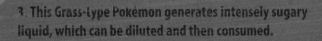
3. This Grass-type Pokémon generates intensely sugary liquid, which can be diluted and then consumed.

4. This Pokémon was created when a child playing on a beach created a mound of sand.

5. These Grass-type Pokémon are sometimes used in beauty salon advertising.

ANSWERS ON PAGE 92

RING AROUND THE COLORS

Many Pokémon on Akala Island are bright and bold—and the dazzling colors make them kind of hard to remember. But you are not fazed by this—you know their specific colorations better than most. Using the illustration below, see if you can guess the missing color on Comfey by picking from the options on the left. You can do this!

OPTIONS:

Blue

Red

Yellow

Green

ANSWER ON PAGE 92

EVOLUTION REVOLUTION

Oranguru is a little jealous of Pokémon that evolve—since it does not. Help Oranguru feel better about itself and identify if the following are real Evolutions or fabrications! Mark them true or false, then check the answer key to see if you're a true Pokémon expert!

		True	False
1	Passimian evolves into Oranguru	◯	◯
2	Palossand is the final Evolution of Sandygast	◯	◯
3	Steenee evolves into Bounsweet	◯	◯
4	Fomantis evolves into Tsareena	◯	◯
5	Mareanie evolves into Toxapex	◯	◯
6	Dewpider evolves into Araquanid	◯	◯
7	Salazzle evolves into Salandit	◯	◯
8	Comfey does not evolve	◯	◯

ANSWERS ON PAGE 92

AKALA ISLAND

CROSSWORD

Another missing Pokémon? Some of these Trainers are just not paying attention! Help out by completing this crossword puzzle, and somewhere in the answer you'll find the missing Pokémon!

ACROSS

1. This Pokémon can spew out its innards to strike opponents.
6. This Fire- and Ghost-type Pokémon wields a flaming bone that is protected by its mother's spirit.
7. Oranguru's two types are Normal and _ _ _ _ _ _.

DOWN

1. In order to evolve, this Ghost- and Ground-type Pokémon took control of people playing in the sand to build up its body.
2. This Fighting type hangs out in groups of about 20, and shares a remarkably strong bond—and was recently lost by a careless Trainer!
3. Some Trainers enthusiastically accept the challenge of keeping this Pokémon's coloring bright and vivid.
4. Toxapex is a Poison- and _ _ _ _ _ -type Pokémon that has poisonous effects that linger for three very painful days.
5. This Pokémon attacks with its head spike which delivers poison that can weaken a foe.

Thanks to you, we found our Pokémon! It was _ _ _ _ _ _ _ _ _ _ _ _ _ _ _ _ _ _ _ !

ANSWERS ON PAGE 92

IT TAKES ALL TYPES

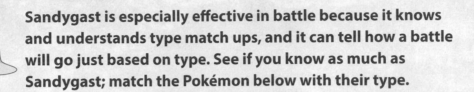

Sandygast is especially effective in battle because it knows and understands type match ups, and it can tell how a battle will go just based on type. See if you know as much as Sandygast; match the Pokémon below with their type.

FIRE
GHOST

GRASS

NORMAL
PSYCHIC

FAIRY

WATER
BUG

POISON
FIRE

ANSWERS ON PAGE 92

TIME TRAVELER

Palossand loves the beach. When the crowds begin to form during the day, Palossand may decide to wait until daylight comes before it ventures out. Play this time-based game and tell us whether you'll see Palossand in the daylight or by moonlight!

You have until 6:00 A.M. to catch Palossand by moonlight.

At ten minutes past midnight, you venture out.

Three hours later, you finally spot a Palossand.

You wait for at least 45 minutes until you approach it, Poké Ball at the ready!

After a fierce 90-minute confrontation, you finally befriend Palossand.

Five minutes later, you feel a weird psychic wave flow over you.

Ten minutes after that, you see Palossand by your side.

Did you catch Palossand by moonlight, or in daylight?

ANSWER ON PAGE 93

COUNT ON IT
PYUKUMUKU

How many Pyukumuku does it take to change a light bulb? None, because Pyukumuku can't change light bulbs. Assuming that it needs to scale a cliff of 1,500 feet, approximately how many Pyukumuku will it take, stacked one on top of another, to reach the top of the cliff? Check out page 89 for a list of Pokémon heights and weights.

1   500 Pyukumuku

2   1,000 Pyukumuku

3   1,500 Pyukumuku

4   2,000 Pyukumuku

ANSWER ON PAGE 93

AKALA ISLAND

CRYTPOGLYPHICS

Who is the guardian of Akala Island? Decipher the clues below and use the cryptographic to solve this puzzle.

I[T] DR[A]WS [E]N[E]RGY FROM [T]HE

SC[E]N[T] OF F[L]OW[E]RS, [A]ND IS

KNOWN [A]S [T]HE G[U][A]RDI[A]N

OF [A]K[A][L][A] IS[L][A]ND.

_ _ _ _   _ _ _ _

LEGEND

(image)	=T	(image)	=U
(image)	=A	(image)	=L
(image)	=P	(image)	=E

ANSWERS ON PAGE 93

AKALA ISLAND

ULA'ULA
ISLAND

Two out of four islands, and we still have more Pokémon to see in Alola! Some more fascinating Pokémon are still to come, and Ula'ula, in the southeast of the Alola chain, has a ton of them! Welcome to the third island of your journey!

PARTS NOT INCLUDED

Grubbin are always on the lookout for Flying-type Pokémon that love to attack them from overhead. It's why they stick so close to Electric-type Pokémon. But that means Grubbin must quickly identify any Pokémon that are Electric-types to befriend, as well as Flying-types to avoid. Can you identify them just by these pieces, and list what their type is?

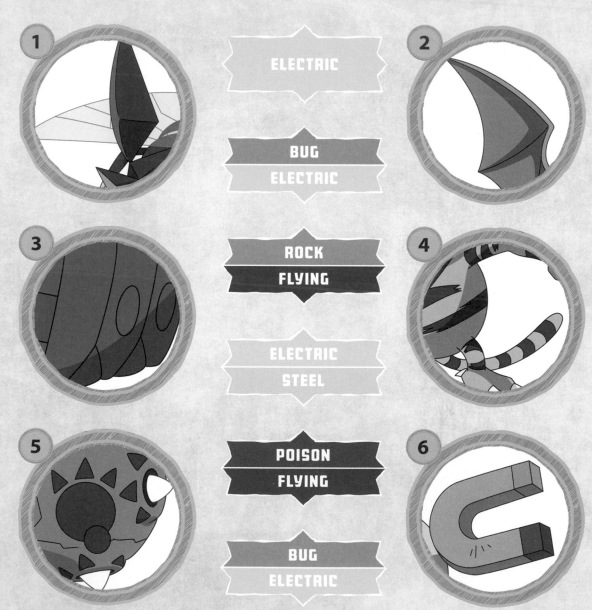

1

2

ELECTRIC

BUG
ELECTRIC

3

4

ROCK
FLYING

ELECTRIC
STEEL

5

6

POISON
FLYING

BUG
ELECTRIC

ANSWERS ON PAGE 93

POKÉMON ACROSTICS

Charjabug wants to play a game to see how well you know your Pokémon names. Play this game with one, two, or three players.

RULES

Pick a Pokémon name. Write the name in a column. If you pick a Pokémon like Charjabug, you should have a column that looks like this. Now, spell the longest word you can with the letters in each row. For example, starting with the first letter, try to spell the longest word you can with C like "compatibility". You can only make one word per row, and you get a point for each letter in the word.

C _____

H _____

A _____

R _____

J _____

A _____

B _____

U _____

G _____

BONUS: Time the game and see how many words you can make in two minutes. Give yourself an extra five points per line for spelling Pokémon names!

FINISH THIS POKÉMON

ULA'ULA ISLAND

Sometimes it's hard to get a good glimpse of Vikavolt with all that electricity flowing from its body. Let's see how much your eyes have retained. Finish drawing this Vikavolt—and then you can pick the correct color combination to complete it!

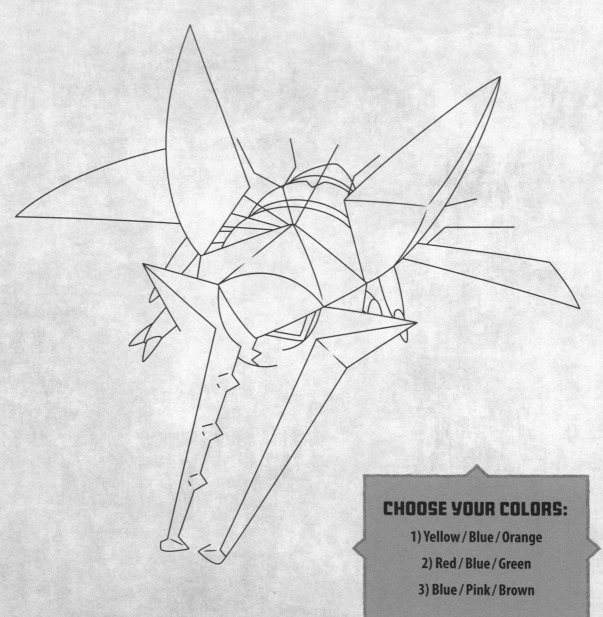

CHOOSE YOUR COLORS:

1) Yellow / Blue / Orange

2) Red / Blue / Green

3) Blue / Pink / Brown

ANSWER ON PAGE 93

ODD POKÉMON OUT

Alolan Grimer developed in the Alola region after it was called upon to deal with a persistent garbage problem. Now that it has some dangerous toxins under control, see if you can help it identify when a Pokémon is in the wrong type group. The three clues below identify a certain type. Find out the type, then circle the Pokémon that belongs to that type from the list below. Time yourself to see if you can help Alolan Grimer quickly clean up this mystery in Alola.

1 • Someone can put one in your ear when spreading rumors
- This is what happens when something "bothers" you
- It can also mean a small listening device

ANSWER: _____
Which of these Pokémon have this as its type? ▶

2 • If you're not crazy, you're probably this
- It's a level most machinery should operate at
- It can be perceived as boring

ANSWER: _____
Which of these Pokémon have this as one of their types? ▶

3 • You'll need this for a cold drink
- You'll find it at the "poles"
- Too much of it can bring down the mightiest of sea-faring vessels

ANSWER: _____
Which of these Pokémon have this as one of their types? ▶

ANSWERS ON PAGE 93

CROSSWORD

Guess which Pokémon found on Ula'ula Island has two different forms, each one vastly different from the other? The answer is in the crossword below—just look for the Pokémon that is mentioned twice.

ACROSS

2. This Pokémon's combined power is enough to scare away a Gyarardos.
4. A Trainer that likes to go camping would appreciate having this Pokémon as a partner.
6. This Pokémon lives high in the snowy mountains of Alola, where it has developed a shell of thick steel.
7. Though they make their home far away in the mountains, these Pokémon often come into town to visit and play with local children.
8. This Pokémon lives in a permanent state of sleep, cuddling its precious log or its Trainer's arm.

DOWN

1. If this Pokémon looks like it's about to cry, watch out! The light that shines from its watering draws the entire school.
3. Togedemaru's types includes Electric and _ _ _ _ _ _.
5. Poisonous gases and flames spew from this Pokémon's nostrils.

Thanks to you, we found our Pokémon! It was __ __ __ __ __ __ __ __ __ __ __ __ __ __ !

WORD SCRAMBLE

Help us identify a mysterious Pokémon that is lurking in the forests and tall grass of Ula'ula Island. Unscramble these clues, and then take the highlighted letters in each clue to discover its name!

THE SPORES THAT THIS POKÉ☐ON GIVES OFF

FLICKER WITH A HYPNOTIC LIGHT THAT

SENDS VIEWERS TO SL☐EP. DURING THE DAY,

IT P☐ANTS ITSE☐F BESIDE A T☐EE

TO ABSORB N☐TRIENTS FROM THE RO☐TS

WHI☐E IT NAPS.

☐ ☐ ☐ ☐ ☐ ☐ ☐ ☐

ANSWERS ON PAGE 93

SPOT THE DIFFERENCE

Did you see the elusive Minior? Which one? You know that Minior appears in several forms, right? Whether in Meteor Form or Red Core, you should be able to spot the differences between the real Pokémon and fake ones. See if you can spot the real forms of Minior in this group below.

ULA'ULA ISLAND

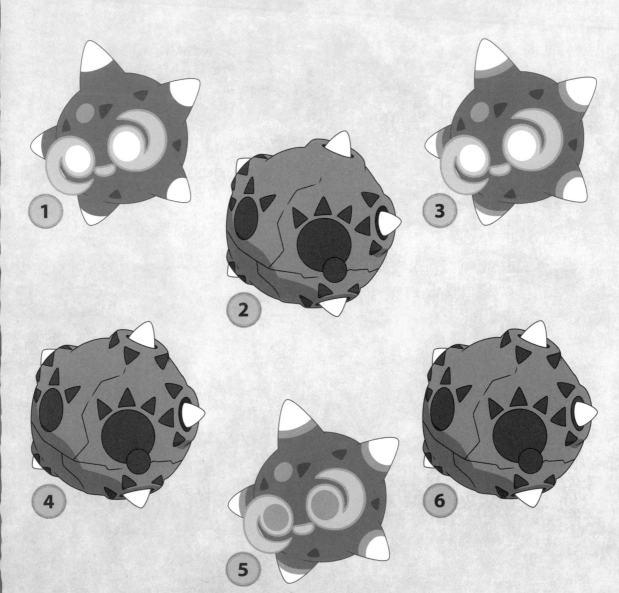

ANSWERS ON PAGE 93

WHO'S THAT POKÉMON?

Komala never wakes up, because it's always in a permanent state of sleep. But in its dreams, it can still identify Pokémon. Help Komala go from fuzzy headed to quick witted by identifying these Pokémon as fast as you can!

9

10

ANSWERS ON PAGE 93

ULA'ULA ISLAND

MATCH THE TYPE

Turtonator can be tricky to battle with—you must find the hole in its stomach to do any real damage. That said, Turtonator also knows exactly what to expect from its opponents. Do you? See if you can match the type with the dual-type Pokémon below.

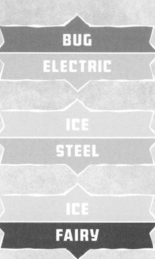

BUG / ELECTRIC

ICE / STEEL

ICE / FAIRY

ROCK / ELECTRIC

NORMAL / DRAGON

POISON / DARK

GHOST / FAIRY

ULA'ULA ISLAND

ANSWERS ON PAGE 93

RING AROUND THE COLORS

Think you can spot Togedemaru before it strikes with its electric attacks? Once you're blinded by all that dazzling light, can you remember what colors made up its look? Let's see—identify the missing color from Togedemaru by picking from the list below.

OPTIONS:

Green

Red

Blue

Yellow

ANSWER ON PAGE 94

MAZE ME

Alolan Geodude, Graveler, and Golem need to leave Ula'ula Island, for a rock reunion with some of their other Pokémon friends. The problem is—navigating through the island is tricky! Help Geodude find Graveler, and then pick up Golem on your way out and get ready for a stone-cold blast!

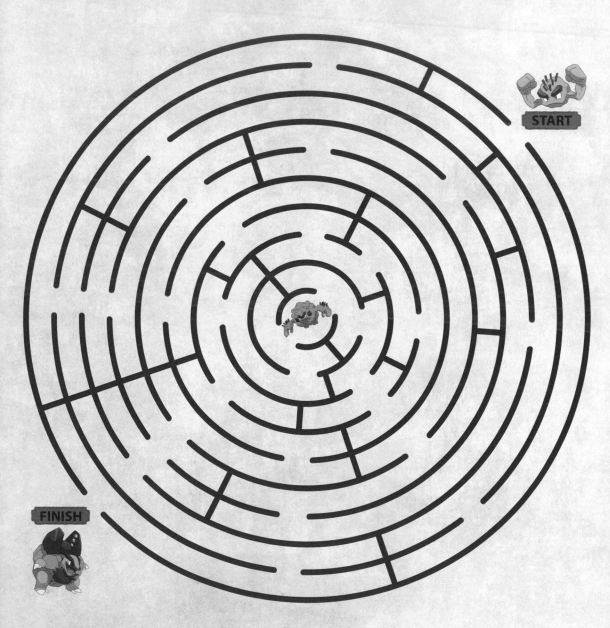

START

FINISH

ANSWERS ON PAGE 94

ODD POKÉMON OUT

Mimikyu hides underneath an old rag so it doesn't scare anyone while it's trying to make friends. See if you can help Mimikyu make some Pokémon friends. Pick out which of the following Pokémon share one of Mimikyu's types!

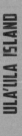

ANSWERS ON PAGE 94

FIND THAT POKÉMON!

There's an elusive Pokémon we've been excited to train—the problem is, we can't find it anywhere. Maybe you can help! Solve this crossword, and the Pokémon mentioned twice is the Pokémon we're looking for!

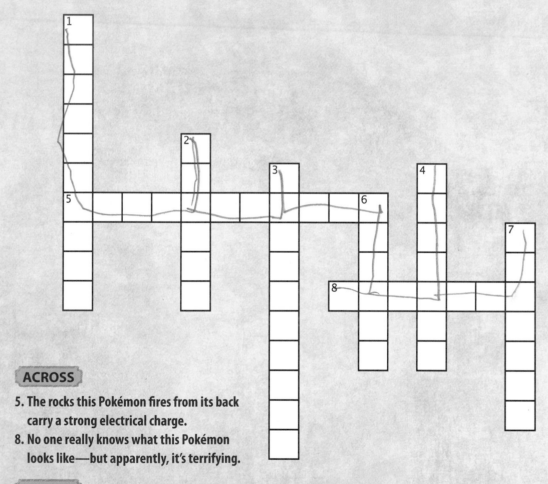

ACROSS

5. The rocks this Pokémon fires from its back carry a strong electrical charge.
8. No one really knows what this Pokémon looks like—but apparently, it's terrifying.

DOWN

1. Its shell is made of unstable material that might explode upon impact.
2. These Pokémon have a real soft spot for kids.
3. Its back is covered with long, spiny fur that usually lies flat.
4. Don't let the beguiling grin of this Pokémon fool you – those teeth are sharp and strong!
6. The atmospheric dust that this Pokémon consumes influences the color of its core.
7. This Pokémon can wield psychic powers mighty enough to stun an opponent in battle.

Thanks to you, we found our Pokémon! It was ___ ___ ___ ___ ___ ___ ___ ___ ___ !

ANSWERS ON PAGE 94

POKÉMON ACROSTICS

Once again, let's see how creative you can be with Pokémon names. Play this game with one, two, or three players.

RULES

Pick a Pokémon name. Write the name in a column. If you pick a Pokémon like Drampa, you should have a column that looks like this. Now, spell the longest word you can with the letters in each row. For example, starting with the first letter, try to spell the longest word you can with D like "delicatessen". You can only make one word per row, and you get a point for each letter in the word.

D _____

R _____

A _____

M _____

P _____

A _____

BONUS: Time the game and see how many words you can make in two minutes. Give yourself an extra five points per line for spelling Pokémon names!

TIME TRAVELER

Alolan Sandshrew is part of a Sandshrew-sliding contest for a festival and needs to make it to the contest by 6:00 P.M. before it gets too cold. Let's find out if this Sandshrew was able to slide on the ice right into the contest on time!

It started out sliding around at 9:30 A.M. in the morning on the festival grounds.

2.5 hours later, it began to forage for food and wandered far into the mountains.

It took 75 minutes for it to eat.

After a short nap of 30 minutes, it began to head back toward the festival grounds.

90 minutes into its journey, it stopped for a rest.

It rested 45 minutes, and trekked out once again.

60 minutes later it could see the festival grounds!

25 minutes after spotting the contest area, it was resting comfortably at the contest starting line.

Did Alolan Sandshrew make it to the contest before 6:00 P.M.?

ANSWER ON PAGE 94

PARTS NOT INCLUDED

Alolan Vulpix has adapted itself for snowy climates, but that hasn't stopped it from being a sharp identifier of fellow Pokémon. See if you're as sharp as Alolan Vulpix and can name the Pokémon seen on Ula'ula Island below just from their appendages or coloring!

1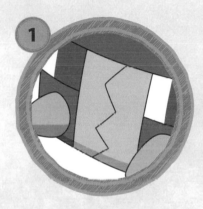

2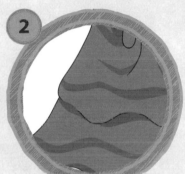

3

_____ _____ _____

4

5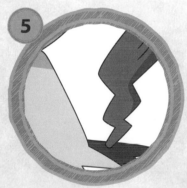

6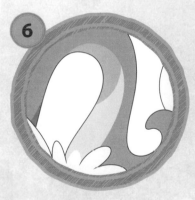

_____ _____ _____

ANSWERS ON PAGE 94

ULA'ULA ISLAND

CODE POKÉMON

So, who's the guardian tapu of Ula'ula Island? We can tell you this—it has a reputation for laziness, commanding vines to pin down foes rather than battling directly, and it absorbs energy from the plants that grow in its wake. The answer is hidden in the puzzle below. Color all the letters that have Alolan Pokémon, and it will spell out that Tapu you seek.

I A P U B U L U

ANSWERS ON PAGE 94

PONI
ISLAND

The fourth island of Alola is the southwestern Poni Island. With a lot of nature on this island, you're sure to discover some terrific Pokémon. The Pokémon found on Poni Island include new Dragon types, and old favorites with a new twist like Alolan Exeggutor.

POKÉMON NAME GAME

Crabrawler is always looking for a fight—and it has the pincers to back it up! But it also knows that it needs a sharp mind as well as pointy claws to win a battle, and it keeps its wits keen by playing the Name Game. Challenge Crabrawler with this one-player, two-player, or multiplayer game—but try not to make it angry!

RULES

You and a friend pick out a Pokémon, like Crabrawler. Each of you then writes the Pokémon name down on a piece of paper. Now come up with as many words as you can, using that Pokémon's letters within a two-minute time limit. The player with the most words after two minutes wins.

Example:
CRABRAWLER

Crab

Brawl

Bale

Brew

Crew

POKÉMON SEEK AND FIND

Poni Island is full of mystery and intrigue and hard-to-catch Pokémon! We're looking for one particularly elusive Pokémon, whose name escapes us right now, but can be found in the following word search. Find these Pokémon, and then take the red highlighted letters and unscramble them to find the Pokémon we seek. Good luck!

```
L H G E Y V N S R W F P M R R B U V Z V A J W
R X D G N M F A P L X T C R A I Y S U L C Z U
G M V F C W E C D I Q O A X L R B Q G Y S O B
Z B F F U W R O C K R U F F O W S O K X B F Z
Z X P O E F X Q C N O W N L L V K S M W J Q L
W A U B A L R L A V S P Q B A A S O W B G Z N
D O A Q Z Q J C K Y R P V D N X F K R Z E S H
Y R J K A I Y J B P Q E H M D L L B P U T E S
H I V T E L A Z Q O O X S N I D G P Q I L C A
U C R A B O M I N A B L E Y G S Y C B U D R A
N O O I R H Q B C O C I W C L H T M A Y M A J
K R C Q A R E Z Q H U P D Z E M P U F N M B T
C I K C L M H U H T T M R Q T U B D F D N R X
F O R W D I K V E R I S G H T D P S D F P A J
X C U K L S Y O K E E D E Q X B G D I Z U W A
C M F Z I P K P D U F I H F Z R G A Y Q G L A
L F F A K K Q U B Z L H Y R M A J L X C E E B
D D I K Z M J Q K M Y M W X V Y T E V M O R F
```

ROCKRUFF   **RIBOMBEE**   **CUTIEFLY**   **BEWEAR**
ORICORIO   **ROCKRUFF**   **LYCANROC**   **STUFFUL**
MUDSDALE   **MUDBRAY**   **CRABRAWLER**   **ALOLAN DIGLETT**

Our missing Pokémon was ___ ___ ___ ___ ___ ___ ___ ___ ___ ___ ___

ANSWERS ON PAGE 94

POKÉMON CHECKLIST

Do you have everything you need to explore Poni Island? Poké Balls? Backpack? Pokédex? If you want to find an Alolan Diglett, you'd better make sure you have the following items on this checklist. See if you can find the items in the collage below:

CHECKLIST

- [ ] Rotom Pokédex
- [ ] Oran Berry
- [ ] Pecha Berry
- [ ] Sitrus Berry
- [ ] Tamato Berry
- [ ] Poké Ball

ANSWERS ON PAGE 94

PONI ISLAND

SPOT THE DIFFERENCE

Oricorio is an odd one—not only does it show up in four different styles, but it's hard to tell when something is wrong because the styles are so flamboyant! But you can do this. First, identify each style, then see if you can spot the fakes among the real Oricorio. Time yourself for a real challenge.

ANSWERS ON PAGE 95

RING AROUND THE COLORS

Cutiefly puts the "cute" in … well, you get where we're going with this adorable Pokémon. But can you identify one of these brightly colored Pokémon minus some of its distinctive colors? See if you can remember what color Cutiefly is missing by checking off the box to the left.

OPTIONS:

Peach

Pink

Tan

Gray

ANSWER ON PAGE 95

FINISH THIS POKÉMON

Okay, let's try something a little harder. Not only do you have to finish drawing this Ribombee from memory, but you have to call out the three missing colors from its illustration. Want an extra challenge? Try to finish this drawing in under 30 seconds!

CHOOSE THE MISSING COLORS:

1) Tan, Brown, and Yellow

2) Blue, Green, and Tan

3) Yellow, Brown, and Blue

4) Pink, Green, and Gray

ANSWER ON PAGE 95

MAZE ME

Rockruff has a long history of living in harmony with people, and many Trainers would find themselves in good company with a Rockruff at their side. Help this Rockruff find its way through this maze on Poni Island so it can join you on your journey!

START

FINISH

ANSWER ON PAGE 95

IT TAKES ALL TYPES

Despite its looks, Lycanroc is fiercely loyal to its Trainer. Lycanroc is a good battler. One way that it helps in battles is to identify the types of Pokémon it meets on the island. See if you can draw a line from the Pokémon on the left to its correct type on the right. Then circle the two Pokémon from each group that match types! Use green markers or crayons for grass, blue for water, and orange for fire—and be careful—all of these are dual-types!

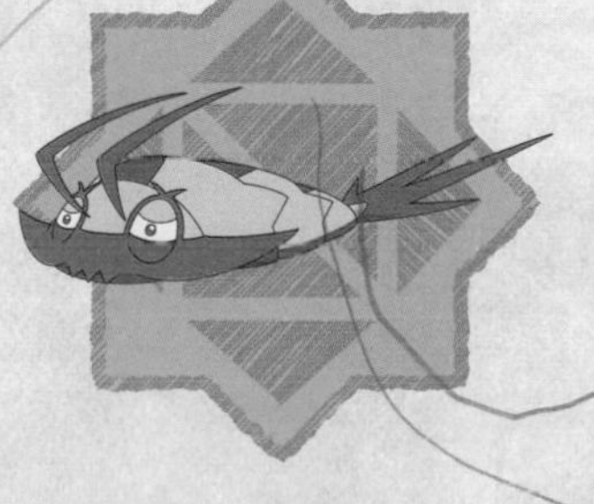

NORMAL

GHOST

DRAGON

GRASS

FIGHTING

BUG

WATER

ANSWERS ON PAGE 95

TIME TRAVELER

Mudbray is a fun-loving Ground-type Pokémon that loves playing in the mud. The mud gives it better traction for running. See if Mudbray can get enough mud to run all day and be back before the sun sets at 6:00 P.M.

Mudbray is spotted at 3:15 P.M.

A Trainer catches Mudbray after much difficulty. Catching Mudbray takes 45 minutes.

The Trainer feeds Mudbray which takes a half hour.

15 minutes later, Mudbray is ready to train again.

Mudbray splashes around in the mud for another twenty minutes.

Mudbray takes a twenty-minute nap.

When Mudbray awakens, it starts on a journey to the nearest Pokémon Center to heal.

That takes one hour and five minutes to make the journey there and back.

Did Mudbray make it back before the end of day?

ANSWER ON PAGE 95

WHO'S THAT POKÉMON

You thought Mudbray was trouble, playing in the mud all day, wait until you get a load of Mudsdale. At 8'02" tall and weighing over 2,000 pounds, Mudsdale is so powerful that it can deliver heavy kicks powerful enough to demolish a big truck. But with all that power Mudsdale still needs to be sharp-witted—like making sure that it can spot its opponents in the blink of a horse's eye. See if you can do the same by identifying these Pokémon by their silhouettes.

1

2

3

4

5

6

ANSWERS ON PAGE 95

PONI ISLAND

WORD SEARCH

PONI ISLAND

Another beautiful day in paradise, and another Pokémon gone missing. Help us find this Pokémon by unearthing all the following Pokémon in the word search below, then taking the red highlighted letters and unscrambling them to identify our missing Pokémon!

```
E K I Q K H U L S V K S N D C H H Y J C
V H H W Z T U T T W V V R J L Y P Y K S
A H E O Z X Z E U X U G X P D C U Y L J
L L D T J T Y V F Q R O C K R U F F P G
J Q O A C D Z O F H G Z W F K T Y B Y V
P G C L P G G L U F O U Y G S I K O Z V
C C P W A W B J L M Q R F O M E G T F I
P X S S K N F G Q P S X W L U F I D K M
R V D P L X D X M E K O M I D L B F H M
V P C A S H F U S G C D F S B Y Z X C O
C Y A X N Z J I G W K F K I R D K R R R
G C H E R K M G O T A N P P A S R W G Q
M O G K W L G V T O R B J O Y X K V O Z
R U S M E A S H Q N M I G D M N G F S Q
L G B H N N W V S W N P O F W F R O H G
B I D D R S Q J M E K P Q F M D P R B D
A L O L A N E X E G G U T O R Y L L D M
```

GOLISIPOD   **ALOLAN DUGTRIO**   **CUTIEFLY**   **DHELMISE**
ALOLAN EXEGGUTOR   **ROCKRUFF**   **MUDBRAY**

Our missing Pokémon is ___ ___ ___ ___ ___ ___

ANSWERS ON PAGE 95

ODD POKÉMON OUT

Bewear isn't just a name, it's a warning. This super-strong Pokémon tends to deliver bone-crushing hugs as a sign of affection. But as affectionate as Bewear is, it's also very smart. How smart? Smart enough to know which Pokémon belong in which groups. Find the two that belong in each group, circling the correct ones. Then, name them and list their type(s).

1 Which two Pokémon have Dragon as one of their types?

Of the two Pokémon you circled, list:

Name: _____

Type(s): _____

Name: _____

Type(s): _____

2 Which two are only found on Poni Island?

Of the two Pokémon you circled, list:

Name: _____

Type(s): _____

Name: _____

Type(s): _____

3 Which two Pokémon are dual-type Pokémon?

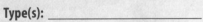

Of the two Pokémon you circled, list:

Name: _____

Type(s): _____

Name: _____

Type(s): _____

Of the Pokémon you circled for each group, which one is the odd one out?

ANSWER: _____

ANSWERS ON PAGE 95

WORD SCRAMBLE

We promise—this is the last time we'll ask for help in finding a missing Pokémon. We lost this one while looking for berries on Poni's south shore. Maybe the clues below will help us decipher who we're looking for. Simply fill in the boxes with the missing letters, and then use the letters to unscramble our Pokémon. Hurry!

WHEN TH□S COWAR□LY POKÉMON

FLEES FRO□ BATTLE, IT LEAVES A □ATH

S□EPT CLEAN BY THE PASSING

□F ITS MANY LEGS.

□ □ □ □ □ □

ANSWER ON PAGE 95

CROSSWORD

Okay, whoops, we lost another one. This time, though, we have some clues about who we're looking for! The clues are all in the crossword puzzle below. Decipher them, and you should have a clearer picture of the Pokémon we need… er, lost!

ACROSS

1. This is one of its types.
6. It lives quietly in _ _ _ _ _ _ _ _ _ _ caves.
8. When the Pokémon we're looking for battles its _ _ _ sharp-clawed arms are certainly up to the task.

DOWN

2. The answer is simply this—it evolves from Answer #7.
3. It meditates and avoids _ _ _ _ _ _ _ _.
4. This is another one of its types.
5. It weighs 238.1 _ _ _ _ _ _.
7. This Pokémon helps keep the beaches and seabed clean while scavenging just about anything edible.

Thanks to you, we found our Pokémon! It was _____!

POKÉMON ACROSTIC

All right, let's see how creative you can be with Pokémon names. Play this game with one, two, or three players.

PONI ISLAND

RULES

Pick a Pokémon name. Write the name in a column. If you pick a Pokémon like Dhelmise, you should have a column that looks like this. Now, spell the longest word you can with the letters in each row. For example, starting with the first letter, try to spell the longest word you can with D like "directional". You can make only one word per row, and you get a point for each letter in the word.

D _____

H _____

E _____

L _____

M _____

I _____

S _____

E _____

BONUS: Time the game and see how many words you can make in two minutes. Give yourself an extra five points per line for spelling Pokémon names!

AN ALL RIGHT HEIGHT

Finding an Alolan Exeggutor may be a tall order, but figuring out how many Pokémon it takes to reach Alolan Exeggutor's height is even harder. Which Pokémon team can you use to get just three inches below Alolan Exeggutor's height? You can only use each Pokémon once. Check out page 89 for a list of Pokémon heights and weights.

TEAM 1	TEAM 2	TEAM 3

ANSWER ON PAGE 96

PONI ISLAND

POKÉMON NAME GAME

Jangmo-o don't interact with a lot of people because of where they live—but they do like playing games with each other. Keep Jangmo-o busy by playing this name game with it. The rules for this one-player, two-player, or multiplayer game are simple.

RULES

You and a friend pick out a Pokémon like Jangmo-o. Each of you then writes that Pokémon name down on a piece of paper. Now come up with as many words as you can using those letters within a two minute limit. The player with the most words after two minutes wins.

BONUS: Use Kommo-o as well, and mix the names together for even more wacky combinations.

Example:

JANGMO-O

Moan

Jog

Moon

Jam

78

SEEK AND FIND

Now we've really done it. We've lost a whole lineup of Pokémon. We desperately need your help to find them. Unfortunately, we can't take every Pokémon we see on Poni Island, so we'll have to settle for only the ones that are Dragon type. Please help us by picking them out from the collage below.

ANSWERS ON PAGE 96

CODE POKÉMON

We're done. We've lost enough Pokémon to last a lifetime. And with your help, we've found most of them. One last request—help us figure out who the guardian of Poni Island is. Color in the letters containing the Pokémon called out below and help us solve the mystery.

_____ _____ _____ _____ _____ _____ _____ _____

ANSWERS ON PAGE 96

LEGENDARY & MYTHICAL POKÉMON

You've finally come to the end of your journey – thank you for visiting Alola. As a parting gift, we'd like to introduce you to some of the Legendary and Mythical Pokémon Alola has to offer—consider yourself lucky if you ever spot one, much less catch and train one!

NAME GAME

Zygarde was originally found in the Kalos region, but it makes a special appearance in Alola. Let's see if you can keep it occupied with this simple name game. The rules for this one-player, two-player or multiplayer game are simple.

RULES

You and a friend pick out a Pokémon like Zygarde. Each of you then writes that Pokémon name down on a piece of paper. Now come up with as many words as you can using that Pokémon letters within a two minute limit. The player with the most words after two minutes wins.

BONUS: Once you've assembled all your words, add the word "Complete" as well, and mix the names together for even more wacky combinations.

Example:

ZYGARDE

Red

Dye

Dry

TAPU TAP TAP MAZE

The guardians of the four islands have lost their way. Can you help each Tapu make it to the correct island they are watching over?

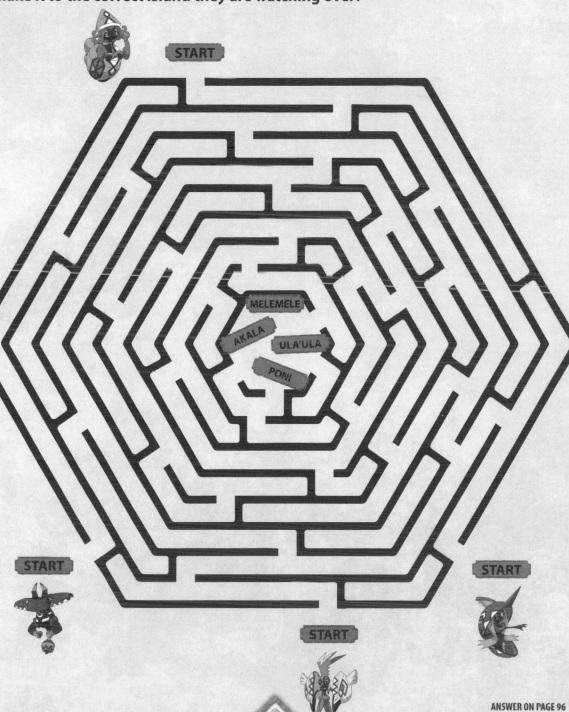

START

START

START

START

MELEMELE

AKALA

ULA'ULA

PONI

ANSWER ON PAGE 96

SPOT THE DIFFERENCE

Cosmog reportedly came to Alola from another world, but its origins are shrouded in mystery. What's not shrouded in mystery is how this Pokémon looks. Find out which Comsog is real and which are posers by identifying the real Cosmog below.

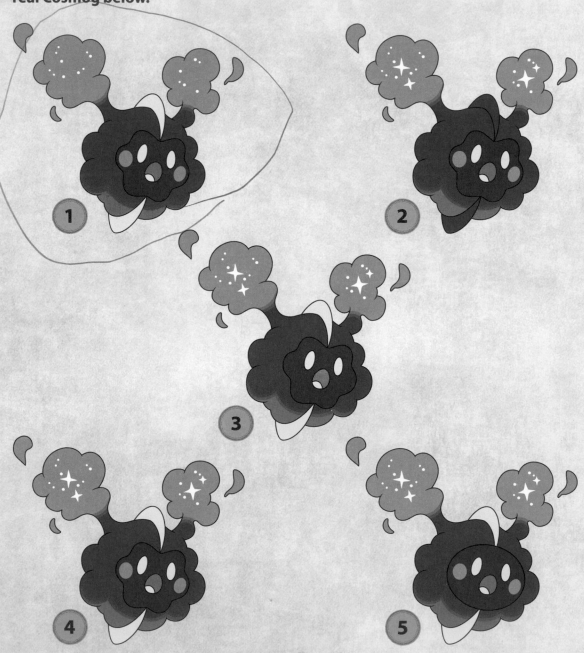

ANSWER ON PAGE 96

LEGENDARY & MYTHICAL POKÉMON

POKÉMON CHECKLIST

Cosmoem never moves, radiating a gentle warmth as it develops inside the hard shell that surrounds it. But you can make a move to get your mind shaped up with this list of some Legendary and Mythical Pokémon stats. You just match the Pokémon on the left to their stats on the right. Good luck! If you're stuck, check page 89.

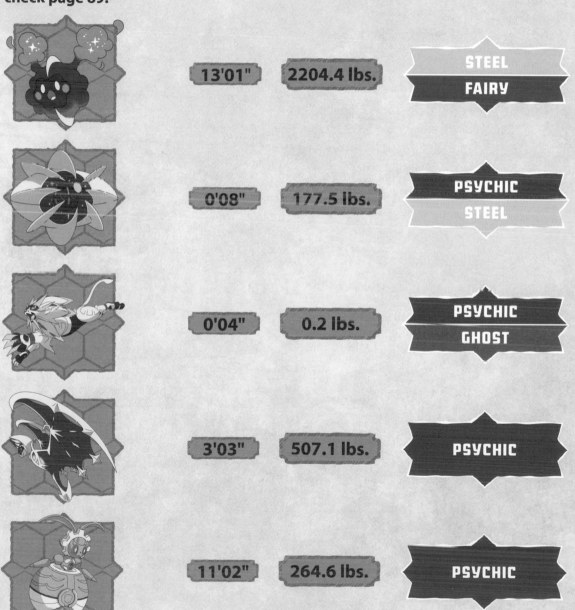

13'01" **2204.4 lbs.** STEEL / FAIRY

0'08" **177.5 lbs.** PSYCHIC / STEEL

0'04" **0.2 lbs.** PSYCHIC / GHOST

3'03" **507.1 lbs.** PSYCHIC

11'02" **264.6 lbs.** PSYCHIC

ANSWERS ON PAGE 96

MATCH THE MOVE

Yes, Legendary and Mythical Pokémon have skills. Some of them you probably don't want to know about when facing them in battle. Others are great to have in your pocket when facing formidable foes. See if you can match the move with the Legendary Pokémon below—there are more than one move for each, so draw a circle around the move, and then a line (or multiple lines) to the moves on the right!

SPLASH

COSMIC POWER

TELEPORT

MOONGEIST BEAM

SUNSTEEL STRIKE

COSMIC POWER

WAKE-UP SLAP

METAL CLAW

HYPNOSIS

CONFUSION

ANSWERS ON PAGE 96

POKÉMON LEGENDARY WALL SCRAWL

We found a message in a bottle washed up on one of the beaches in the Alola region. Someone was obviously trying to let us know that they found a treasure trove of Pokémon. See if you can decipher which Pokémon they're talking about!

CAUSE MOE M

SOUL GA LAY O

LOU NALL UH

ZAI GAR D

KOZ MAWG

ANSWERS ON PAGE 96

CRYPTOGLYPHICS

Can you help us find out who this mysterious Mythical Pokémon is? Decipher the clues below and use the cryptographic to solve this puzzle. But just to make things harder, we replaced letters with whole words. You can do it!

IT WAS ___ (Built) MANY ___ (Centuries) AGO BY ___ (Human Inventors).

THE REST OF THIS POKÉMON'S ___ (Mechanical Body) IS

JUST A ___ (Vehicle) FOR ITS ___ (True Self):

THE ___ (Chest) CONTAINED

IN ITS ___ (Soul-Heart). THE MYSTERY

POKÉMON IS:

___ ___ ___ ___ ___ ___ ___ ___

LEGEND

	= Vehicle
	= True Self
	= Built
	= Chest
	= Mechanical Body
	= Human Inventors
	= Soul-Heart
	= Centuries

ANSWERS ON PAGE 96

LEGENDARY & MYTHICAL POKÉMON

ALOLA POKÉMON HEIGHT AND WEIGHT REFERENCE CHART

Use the Pokémon heights and weights provided here to complete the activities on previous pages.

Alolan Exeggutor	35'09"	916.2 lbs.	
Alolan Muk	3'03"	114.6 lbs.	
Bewear	6'11"	297.6 lbs.	
Bounsweet	1'00"	7.1 lbs.	
Brionne	2'00"	38.6 lbs.	
Cosmoem	0'04"	2204.4 lbs.	
Cosmog	0'08"	0.2 lbs.	
Crabominabie	5'07"	396.8 lbs.	
Decidueye	5'03"	80.7 lbs.	
Dhelmise	12'10"	463.0 lbs.	
Fomantis	1'00"	3.3 lbs.	
Golisopod	6'07"	238.1 lbs.	
Gumshoos	2'04"	31.3 lbs.	
Incineroar	5'11"	183.0 lbs.	
Kommo-o	5'03"	172.4 lbs.	
Litten	1'04"	9.5 lbs.	
Lunala	13'01"	264.6 lbs.	
Lurantis	2'11"	40.8 lbs.	

Magearna	3'03"	177.5 lbs.	
Morelull	0'08"	3.3 lbs.	
Mudsdale	8'02"	2028.3 lbs.	
Oranguru	4'11"	167.6 lbs.	
Palossand	4'03"	551.2 lbs.	
Passimian	6'07"	182.5 lbs.	
Pikipek	1'00"	2.6 lbs.	
Popplio	1'04"	16.5 lbs.	
Prlmarina	5'11"	97.0 lbs.	
Pyukumuku	1'00"	2.6 lbs.	
Rowlet	1'00"	3.3 lbs.	
Sandygast	1'08"	154.3 lbs.	
Shiinotic	3'03"	25.4 lbs.	
Solgaleo	11'02"	507.1 lbs.	
Steenee	2'04"	18.1 lbs.	
Toucannon	3'07"	57.3 lbs.	
Tsareena	3'11"	47.2 lbs.	

ANSWER KEY

PAGE 6

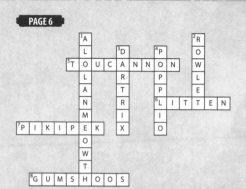

```
          ¹A                    ²R
          L           ³D    ⁴P   O
        ⁵T O U C A N N O N        W
          L           A    P   L
          A           R    P   E
          N           T   ⁶L I T T E N
          M           R    I
          E           I    O
        ⁷P I K I P E K X
          W
          T
        ⁸G U M S H O O S
```

PAGE 7

1. Yungoos   2. Brionne   3. Trumbeak

4. Torracat   5. Alolan Raichu   XDRTAIR = Dartrix

PAGE 8

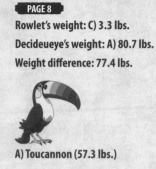

Rowlet's weight: C) 3.3 lbs.

Decideueye's weight: A) 80.7 lbs.

Weight difference: 77.4 lbs.

A) Toucannon (57.3 lbs.)

PAGE 9

Fire-Dark   Dark-Normal   Water-Fairy

Normal-Flying   Grass-Ghost   Water

PAGE 10

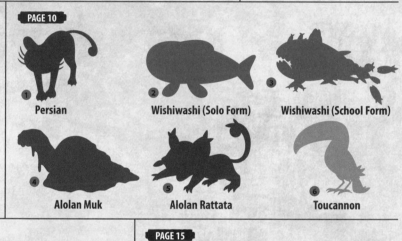

1. Persian   2. Wishiwashi (Solo Form)   3. Wishiwashi (School Form)

4. Alolan Muk   5. Alolan Rattata   6. Toucannon

PAGE 12

Popplio is a Water-type Pokémon.

Wishiwashi (Solo Form)

Pyukumuku

Brionne

PAGE 13

IT PELTS ITS OPPONENTS WITH WATER BALLOONS IN A SWIFT AND SKILLFUL BATTLE DANCE. ITS NAME IS BRIONNE.

PAGE 14

```
U V P T X C U G B N U O U J Z M O W I G
E K F L D R N N O H H K H A L H R G C J
T M O K N O H V A B H O L B D C O P J Y
Y R S T G W F G P R I M A R I N A L C R
T C M T G L O X G T D E C I D U E Y E V
R R T P L E R S E S Z V C E T V U T D
D X P R I T M V D O G K I N W O R N I Z
N R V O C K S O O I T M N T X R G M N H
M F D I P G I H Q S P O C C W R A O U C
J G W N N P S P D K I B I D M A B O C T
G B T P N M L K E R F E N L H C F S D J
R C F L U Y D I B K Q E E Z I A K Z X J
N A N G F C L L O K D C R D G T U N G E
J D A R T R I X M A Z O O L X W T R H G
O J H M U E J H U K R P A R J F J E M O
W X T T V B N Q N N E J R K Z R Z K N V
```

ANSWER: Primarina

PAGE 15

Dartrix   Decideueye

Litten   Torracat   Incineroar

Popplio   Brionne   Primarina

Pikipek   Trumbeak   Toucannon

ANSWER: Pikipek

90

PAGE 16

10 Primarina
(970 lbs.)

PAGE 17

Blue

PAGE 18

④

PAGE 19

ANSWER: No, the Gumshoos is asleep. It's 6:05 P.M.

PAGE 20

① ② ③ ④ ⑤ ⑥

PAGE 22

① Decidueye

② Primarina

③ Alolan Raticate

④ Alolan Persian

⑤ Alolan Muk

⑥ Trumbeak

PAGE 24

MAREANIE

ANSWER: Mareanie

PAGE 25

1. Fomantis   2. Araquanid   3. Salazzle

4. Alolan Marowak   5. Steenee   EAXXPOT = Toxapex

PAGE 26

Dewpider:
1) Green / Blue / Gray

PAGE 27

④ Oranguru 167.6 lbs.   Passimian 182.5 lbs.

Together that's 350.1 lbs.

PAGE 29

SHY KNOT ECK = Shiinotic

DO PIE DER = Dewpider

PASS IM EYAN = Passimian

PAHL O SAND = Palossand

SAL AZ EL = Salazzle

LOOR RANT IZ = Lurantis

PAGE 28

1. Shiinotic   2. Salandit   3. Steenee   4. Comfey

5. Oranguru   6. Pyukumuku   7. Fomantis

PAGE 30

Salazzle   Shiinotic   Oranguru   Lurantis

Passimian   Araquanid   Palossand

PAGE 31

Salazzle is a Poison- and Fire-type Pokémon.

Toxapex
Poison-Water

Alolan Marowak
Fire-Ghost

PAGE 32

1 Oranguru

2 Palossand

3 Steenee

4 Toxapex

5 Mareanie

6 Lurantis

7 Pyukumuku

8 Comfey

9 Dewpider

PAGE 33

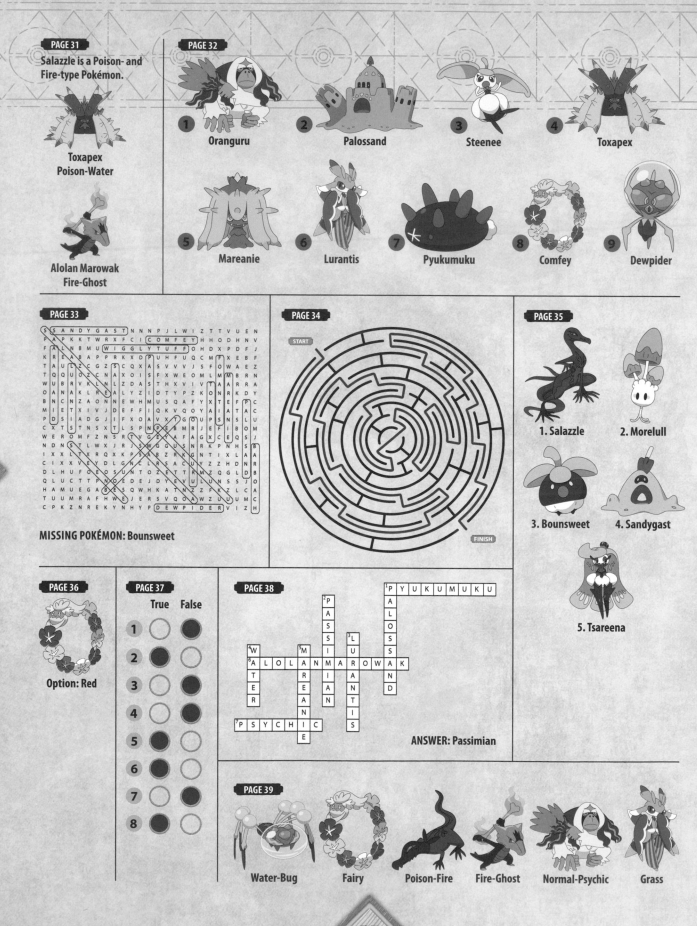

MISSING POKÉMON: Bounsweet

PAGE 34

START

FINISH

PAGE 35

1. Salazzle

2. Morelull

3. Bounsweet

4. Sandygast

5. Tsareena

PAGE 36

Option: Red

PAGE 37

	True	False
1	○	●
2	●	○
3	○	●
4	○	●
5	●	○
6	●	○
7	○	●
8	●	○

PAGE 38

ANSWER: Passimian

PAGE 39

Water-Bug

Fairy

Poison-Fire

Fire-Ghost

Normal-Psychic

Grass

PAGE 40

ANSWER: You caught Palossand by moonlight!

PAGE 41

3

1,500 Pyukumuku

PAGE 40

IT DRAWS ENERGY FROM THE SCENT OF FLOWERS, AND IS KNOWN AS THE GUARDIAN OF AKALA ISLAND. TAPU LELE

PAGE 44

1 **Vikavolt** Bug-Electric

2 **Golbat** Poison-Flying

3 **Charjabug** Bug-Electric

4 **Electabuzz** Electric

5 **Minior (Meteor)** Rock-Flying

6 **Magnemite** Electric-Steel

PAGE 46

Vikavolt
1) Yellow / Blue / Orange

PAGE 47

Bug

1 **Grubbin**

Normal

2

Ice

3 **Alolan Vulpix**

PAGE 48

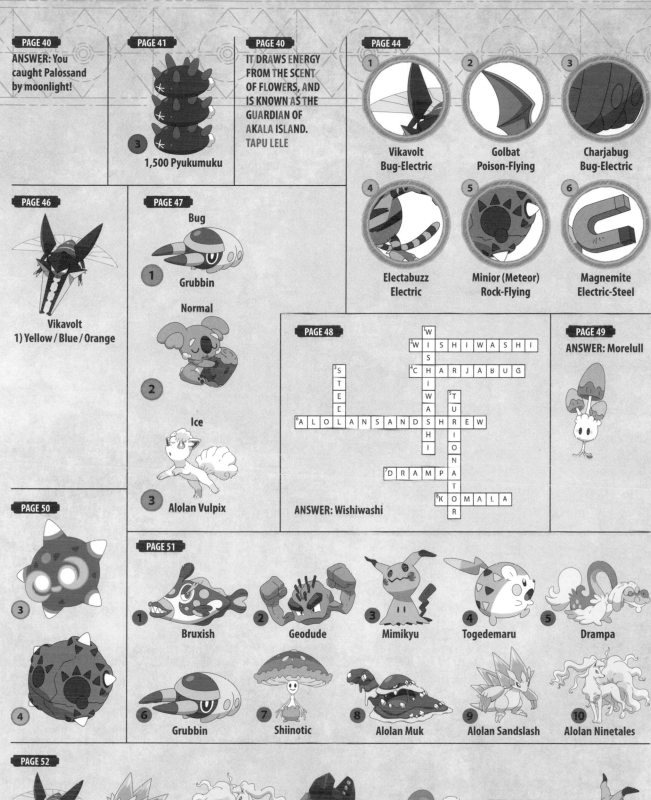

```
        ¹W
      ²W I S H I W A S H I
    ³S   S   ⁴C H A R J A B U G
    T    H           I
    E    I          ⁵T
    E    W          U
  ⁶A L O L A N S A N D S H R E W
         S           I
         H           O
         I           N
                     A
                    ⁷D R A M P A
                     O
                    ⁸K O M A L A
                     R
```

ANSWER: Wishiwashi

PAGE 49

ANSWER: Morelull

PAGE 50

3

4

PAGE 51

1 **Bruxish**

2 **Geodude**

3 **Mimikyu**

4 **Togedemaru**

5 **Drampa**

6 **Grubbin**

7 **Shiinotic**

8 **Alolan Muk**

9 **Alolan Sandslash**

10 **Alolan Ninetales**

PAGE 52

Vikavolt Bug-electric

Alolan Sandslash Ice-Steel

Alolan Ninetales Ice-Fairy

Alolan Golem Rock-Electric

Drampa Normal-Dragon

Alolan Muk Poison-Dark

Mimikyu Ghost-Fairy

PAGE 53

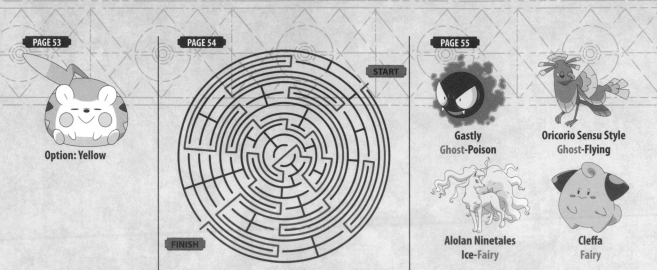

Option: Yellow

PAGE 54

START

FINISH

PAGE 55

Gastly
Ghost-Poison

Oricorio Sensu Style
Ghost-Flying

Alolan Ninetales
Ice-Fairy

Cleffa
Fairy

PAGE 56

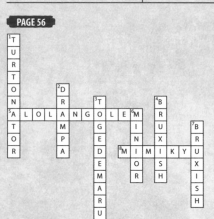

ANSWER: Bruxish

PAGE 58

ANSWER: Yes. Alolan Sandshrew slid into the test by 5:25 P.M.

PAGE 59

1 Charjabug

2 Alolan Grimer

3 Wishiwashi (School Form)

4

5 Mimikyu

6 Drampa

PAGE 60

ANSWER: Tapu Bulu

PAGE 63

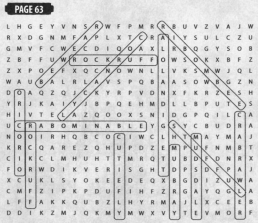

MISSING POKÉMON: Crabominable

PAGE 64

Rotom
Pokédex

Oran
Berry

Pecha
Berry

Sitrus
Berry

Tamato
Berry

Poké
Ball

PAGE 65

3 5 10 11

PAGE 66

Option: Tan

PAGE 67

Ribombee:
1) Tan, Brown, and Yellow

PAGE 68

PAGE 69

Hakamo-o
Dragon-Fighting

Dhelmise
Ghost-Grass

Alolan Exeggutor
Grass-Dragon

Wimpod
Bug-Water

Bewear
Normal-Fighting

PAGE 70

ANSWER: No, Mudbray was exhausted
and didn't get back until 6:30 P.M.

PAGE 71

1 Alolan Exeggutor

2 Lycanroc (Midnight Form)

3 Oricorio (Pa'u Style)

4 Ribombee

5 Crabrawler

6 Crabominable

PAGE 72

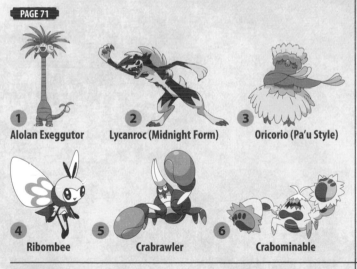

MISSING POKÉMON: Stufful

PAGE 73

1) Kommo-o: Dragon-Fighting
Alolan Exeggutor: Grass-Dragon

2) Dhelmise: Ghost-Grass
Jangmo-o: Dragon

3) Exeggcute: Grass-Psychic
Hakamo-o: Dragon-Fighting

ANSWER: Jangmo-o is the only pure Dragon type.

PAGE 74

Wimpod

PAGE 75

ANSWER:
Golisopod

PAGE 77 Team 1:

12'10"   8'02"   6'11"   6'07"   1'00"

PAGE 79

Alolan Exeggutor   Hakamo-o   Jangmo-o

PAGE 80

TAPU FINI

ANSWER: Tapu Fini

PAGE 83

- Tapu Koko: Melemele Island
- Tapu Lele: Akala Island
- Tapu Bulu: Ula'ula Island
- Tapu Fini: Poni Island

PAGE 84

4

PAGE 85

| Cosmog
Psychic
0'08"
0.2 lbs. | Cosmoem
Psychic
0'04"
2204.4 lbs. | Solgaleo
Psychic-Steel
11'02"
507.1 lbs. | Lunala
Psychic-Ghost
13'01"
264.6 lbs. | Magearna
Steel-Fairy
3'03"
177.5 lbs. |

PAGE 86

Splash   Sunsteel Strike, Cosmic Power,   Cosmic Power,   Moongeist Beam, Cosmic
           Wake-Up Slap, Teleport,   and Teleport   Power, Hypnosis, Teleport,
           and Metal Claw   and Confusion

PAGE 87

CAUSE MOE M = Cosmoem
SOUL GA LAY O = Solgaleo
LOU NALL UH = Lunala
KOZ MAWG = Cosmog
ZAI GAR D = Zygarde

PAGE 88

It was BUILT many CENTURIES
ago by HUMAN INVENTORS. The rest of
this Pokémon's MECHANICAL BODY is just a
VEHICLE for its TRUE SELF: the SOUL-HEART
contained in its CHEST.
The mystery Pokémon is: Magearna

ROWLET

Use the stickers on the Rowlet page to complete the picture.

LITTEN

Use the stickers on the Litten page to complete the picture.

POPPLIO

Use the stickers on the Popplio page to complete the picture.